Karl Dandenell

Between the Stars
I Found Her

WYLDBLOOD

Published 2025 by Wyldblood Press, Thicket View, Maidenhead SL6 6PX

ISBN 978-1-914417-24-5

Visit www.wyldblood.com for more about our books and magazines and to buy them.

I attended Awusi Osei's funeral in a baseline female clone—essentially a younger version of my original body. A privacy bubble surrounded the funeral party, cutting off everything but our legally mandated emergency data link to the Overmind. The bubble was a luxury I could ill afford these days, but I paid the bill.

Grief is ugly and private. My fans didn't need my red-rimmed eyes and runny nose right then. And I certainly didn't need their commentary about my marriage to Awusi (or our public and messy divorce).

Following the instructions accompanying her suicide note, we'd gathered in a tiny cemetery in Ogooué-Ivindo Province, not far from Ivindo National Park. Awusi and I had exchanged vows in that pristine Gabonese rainforest, our wedding dresses dotted with spray from Djidji waterfall.

Dark, angry clouds were rolling in, bringing a light rain. Two gravediggers, a minister, and an attorney waited nearby, next to an old oak wine barrel filled with black umbrellas. We had more than we needed: I was one of only two mourners present in the flesh. Steven Komori, our first neural net designer, stood at my side, dressed in lacquered samurai armor. Knowing Steven, I suspected he'd borrowed the suit from a museum rather than print out a perfect replica.

Awusi would have appreciated the gesture. Art and impermanence were inextricably linked in her mind. True art, she had told me on more than one occasion, couldn't exist within the Overmind since it remembered *everything* people said or did. Art needs limits, and mistakes, and sometimes failure. If you could resurrect or revise anything, why even bother?

Killing her physical body had been simply the final act of a long, complex performance.

Despite the small number of humans attending, the cemetery was far from empty. Five hundred Overmind avatars, chosen by lottery, shimmered in precise ranks opposite the open grave. Permanent death was sufficiently rare and salacious we'd had to turn away thousands of potential gawkers. Media drones hovered just outside the cemetery's fence like jackals sniffing the edges of a bongo herd.

For the space of forty-five minutes, my entire world consisted of the graveyard and the wind chasing through the okoumé branches.

After the attorney confirmed the erasure of Awusi's medical backups, they lowered her final body into the cold, damp earth, Steven reached over and squeezed my shoulder in a brotherly fashion, his armor clicking. "How are you holding up, Mylene?"

"Badly." I took a shuddering breath and glanced at the empty chairs. "There should be more people here. Christ, she deserves that much, don't you think?"

He glanced at the avatars. "She didn't want any more than this, Mylene."

"I'm not talking about fans wanting to see a *First Uploader*," I said, my voice heavy with irony. She'd never uploaded until the very end, but such facts were lost in the myth. "Where are her students? Her family? *Her lovers?* "It's not like I was the only one still in Earth-Luna."

"Right. Sorry," Steven said. He withdrew his hand and turned his attention to his feet.

Awusi's work in room-temperature superconductors had helped lay the groundwork for the Overmind. Her patents and stock options had made her wealthy, but she donated most of her money and walked away from the project, focusing on dance and poetry.

Well, I walked away, too, I reminded myself.

I wiped my nose and watched the gravediggers shovel dirt over her casket. Then they lit and released a flotilla of balloon lanterns. Each lantern carried one of Awusi's unpublished poems. As soon as the lanterns cleared the perimeter, drones would snatch them from the sky, eager to reveal her final words.

The thought of artistic jackals dissecting her last precious words sat sour in my gut.

"I need to get out of here."

"Okay," Steven said. "Do you want some company? I could lose this armor and meet you for a drink. I think I used to own a bar around here." He laughed, an awkward sound coming from his fierce battle mask.

"I need to write." That's what I told people when I wanted to be alone. It was true, mostly. More to the point, I didn't want to deal with the media drones, even though a quick interview would boost what I still thought of as my bank account.

I handed my umbrella to the minister and walked to a transit station, which took me outside Nairobi, where Gabon hosted its space elevator. Like many people, I'd been surprised when the former French colony won the UN contract over their tech-heavy rival, Kenya. But the public-private partnerships forged by President Raponda had delivered an astonishing piece of engineering safely (and only a few billion Euros over budget).

After I passed through the extensive security screen at the elevator, I took a few hours and updated my personality snapshot, sending the primary data crystal to an archive under the Paris catacombs and the secondary to a former nuclear bunker drilled deep into the Caucasus Mountains.

It wasn't full-proof insurance, I knew. Without my living, breathing body to make a quantum connection, any avatar created from a backup would be little more than clever software, limited to rudimentary interactions. Still, it gave me some comfort, and my credit could cover the maintenance. For now.

Sixteen hours later, I arrived home to *The Flying Dutchman*, which had kept synchronous orbit above

Ayem. The former military vessel greeted me with dimmed lights and a hot bath and didn't engage me in unnecessary conversation. It was good that way.

Back home on *Dutchman*, I wrote. Or at least I tried to write, pushing around words like a frustrated child pushes hated food around her plate. I turned down media requests and let *Dutchman* handle my routine communications. It was far more diplomatic than I was.

There had been a time when I actively courted eyeballs. My lifestyle was expensive—-Awusi and I had spent three hundred million Euros rehabilitating *Dutchman*—which meant I needed to produce music and lectures to keep myself in the public feeds.

Now? Now I couldn't bring myself to care. My current credits would keep me in consumables for another three or four months. Beyond that, I didn't want to think about it. What was the point?

Awusi was *gone*. Not on hiatus. Not hiding away in a restored cabaret club in St. Petersburg. She was in the ground, without even an Avatar left behind.

I forced myself to add some material to the First Uploaders biography. I drafted a bad play. I had *Dutchman* spin up the living module to .999g so I could accurately tune the Steinway and lose myself in Satie's *Gymnopédies*, but the music just brought more tears.

The hours passed without fuss, the ship mirroring the daylight cycle of Amsterdam. *Dutchman*'s drones cleaned around me, heated food, and took away the dirty dishes. I curled up next to an armored porthole for hours, looking over the Sea of Tranquility. Even though the ship was quite warm, I shivered in a wool shawl.

Awusi had been a moon-watcher, and I'd caught the bug from her. She'd dragged me along on camping trips throughout Europe, timing them for the days before the waxing full moon. Three times we rented houses so we could watch eclipses, sitting naked under the sky, sharing kisses and brandy.

Before I met Awusi, I preferred daylight, clear and bright. Sunset made me melancholy. She called me her "anti-vampire."

But even my clear view of sunlit Armstrong City wasn't a good distraction. I was almost grateful when *Dutchman* muted my background music—a solo Bill Evans piano piece—and announced a transmission from Luna.

"What part of 'No calls' don't you understand?" I said, my voice creaky with disuse.

"Your recent instructions didn't specifically exclude your priority list."

"But I *meant*—shit." *Dutchman*'s programming occasionally failed to recognize context, despite my continued tweaking. "Put them through." I stood and stretched, my shoulders popping. The display nearest me opened a video window, hiding my working space of text files, musical scores, and stage designs. A familiar face stared back at me: dark eyes, darker hair pulled back into a complex braid, wide mouth outlined in smoky red: Raadhi Joshi. "Mylene!"

"Hello, young lady."

"Hello yourself, hermit," she said. "I was in the neighborhood, so I thought I'd call."

I glanced back at the porthole, half-expecting to see Raadhi floating there. "That was kind of you. But I'm rather busy."

She pulled her lips into a gentle frown. "So Steven told me."

"Seriously, Raadhi, I'm in the middle of—"

"I have coffee. Roasted first thing."

Raadhi belonged to an extensive coop plantation inside an artificial rainforest in the Pitatus crater. "Bribe accepted. Give me half an hour." I tugged at my sweat-stained shirt. "I could use a shower."

"I'm already en-route. See you in eighteen minutes." She closed the connection.

I managed a quick sponge, changed into a clean shipsuit, and roughly brushed my hair before Raadhi stepped through the airlock. She carried a small bouquet of bright red orchids and a large cloth shopping bag. She smelled of lilacs, as usual.

"For you," she said, handing me the flowers.

"They're lovely. Thank you."

"I have a friend at the spaceport does some wicked things in his hothouse." She flexed her knees. "You know, most people move to orbit to escape gravity."

"It's healthier. And the piano sounds better."

Raadhi shook her head. "True, and it beats making coffee in micro-gee. Galley?"

I pointed. Raadhi strode down the passageway with her bag. "Good morning, *Dutchman*! I need a liter of water at 94 centigrade. And a cafetière."

"Right away, Raadhi. Welcome back."

Five minutes later, Raadhi called. "Come on back, Mylene."

"That smells *amazing*." Raadhi stood to one side of my small dining nook, pouring coffee into large cups of bone china so old their patterns were no more than suggestions. A dish of fresh croissants sat in the middle of the table. She'd even brought linen napkins.

"Please sit," she said, and folded herself into a chair. She waited until I had tasted the coffee and a pastry before filling her own plate. We ate in silence, not out of any sense of awkwardness, but from habit. In the dining hall at the lab, we had a rule the first five minutes of any meal should be focused on eating. No shop talk.

When she had wiped the crumbs from her fingers, Raadhi took a long, slow breath. "I am truly sorry about Awusi. I had great admiration for her."

"Thank you." I nodded and blinked my eyes against the tears lurking there. "She wanted you at the funeral."

"I know," she said. "But one of the rhinos was having a difficult labor. By the time I delivered the calf and flew back from the Botswana preserve... well, it was over and done." She shrugged, a delicate gesture. "Life goes on."

"Not for her," I said, and immediately regretted it.

"She had a good, long life," Raadhi said. "We should honor her decision to end it." Her tone told me this wasn't a topic for debate.

"Of course I honor it. I just wish... Dammit, she might have *asked* my opinion before she committed herself."

"I suspect she already knew what you'd say."

"Maybe. We had a complicated relationship." She was the last person I genuinely loved, and fifty years after the divorce, I still cherished our friendship. Now even that was gone. "You said you'd talked with Steven. How is he?" I asked, trying to shift the conversation.

"He joined a group marriage in Canada. Theater actors, if you can believe that."

Actually, I could. "Good for him," I said with honest affection. "I hope he's happy."

"He seems so. It was a fascinating wedding. The groomsmen arrived via stratospheric free fall jump. One nearly hit the catering tent."

I smiled. "Sorry I missed it. Not the jump," I added. "I'm a little old for that."

"Not at the moment," she said.

"You know what I mean."

Raadhi leaned back and glanced around the galley. I'd programmed random images from the Getty and the Louvre into the bulkhead displays. Fortunately, most of the Getty collection had been digitized before the 2089 earthquake pancaked the building. Interspersed with the Renaissance artists were long, slow videos of farmland in Switzerland, Brazil, and China. "These are lovely," she said. "Did you take them?" She probably knew that I had, but I accepted the conversational opening.

"Some of them." I pointed to a closeup of a sheep nuzzling clover in the mountains outside Zurich. "That won an award. Eighty years ago."

"I remember! Your appearance at the ceremony caused quite a stir."

I had arrived in a black evening gown that did nothing to hide my advanced age. I wasn't completely ancient, but had my share of wrinkles, sun blotches, and liver spots. My white hair was thin, exposing pink skin. Some of the social media commentariat believed I was making a political statement, while others were simply disappointed with my natural state. "If they wanted me to be *vlekkeloos*, they should have specified it in the invitation."

Raadhi blinked up a translation and lifted a corner of her mouth. "But you transferred to a younger clone soon after."

"Well, I'd gotten enough use from that body," I replied. In truth, some of the remarks had brought back an old sense of shame.

"And that's when you got together with Awusi."

I nodded. "We hadn't seen much of each other since the team went its separate ways, and I ran into her in Paris a week after my transition. She'd just finished a long tour with her dance company and was 'gloriously unscheduled.' All she wanted to do was hike and eat chocolate."

"Sounds like a good plan."

"It was," I said. "I had a brand new, strong body, so the two of us walked the Alps and the Pyrenees, sleeping in little village hostels. I thought I was too old to fall in love again. Awusi proved me wrong." The first of many times.

"What a lovely story. Thank you for sharing it," Raadhi said. She folded her napkin and set it in the center of her plate. "So how is the memorial coming along?"

I leaned back and sighed. "Slowly." With a flick of my hand, I brought up my notes and sketches. "It's frustrating. So much of her life is already documented, and two volumes of her autobiography have already been adapted into VR plays."

Raadhi shook her head. "I downloaded the first one. It was pretty... scandalous."

"It was crap," I said sharply. "The director made her out to be some sort of genius sociopath." I had warned Awusi about that. Her manic cycles tended to put people off.

"The public liked it."

"Crap," I repeated. "Though it boosted her rating a few million points."

The problem, I admitted to Raadhi, was trying to find the right way to tell her story. All of it, including the parts no else knew, without sounding cheap or exploitive.

Then I asked the question that had been nagging me.

"Raadhi, you don't suppose this is another performance?" A few decades back, Awusi had disappeared into a "spiritual retreat" for six months, and her inner circle had released a series of carefully cultivated rumors that made it seem like she was dying. In reality, she was creating a new dance company.

"Everything seems aboveboard," she said quietly. "However, I'm willing to look into it, if only to satisfy my own curiosity."

"I appreciate that," I said. "Let me know if you want a contribution."

She shook her head. "My credit is quite healthy these days." Of course it was. Raadhi kept herself busy, working on dozens of eco restoration projects.

"Have you given any thought to what you'll do after you finish the memorial?"

"I don't know, to be honest," I admitted. "Take a sabbatical, maybe."

Raadhi gave me a rich, musical laugh. "Mylene, you've been on sabbatical for the better part of two decades. Maybe three. If you want to retire, then *retire*. Make rum drinks on a beach somewhere. Join a meditation school on Mars. You've certainly earned it."

"That's not for me." I shook my head. "I need to *do* something. And meditation isn't doing something."

"So become a teacher. Or toss it all and go to Rocannan. Raise the family you've always wanted. The colony would be lucky to have you," she said. "Just do anything other than lurk here in your flying Fortress of Solitude. No offense, *Dutchman*."

"None taken," said the ship.

"You barely set foot on Earth," Raadhi continued. "And the only people you talk to are Steven and me."

"Don't forget Evgeni," I said quickly, eager to defend myself.

Raadhi leaned forward. "Mylene, no one's heard from him in almost five years."

"Oh." Had it been that long since we'd spoken? Evgeni was a brilliant scientist, with a curly black beard and a surprising soprano. We first bonded over ridiculous pre-Overmind Russian standup comedians. "He's doing research on Pluto, isn't he?"

"He was. Data packets every day, then nothing. He didn't answer any calls, so we sent drones. They found his station abandoned." She stood and began to clear the dishes. "Everything was clean and packed away. All the equipment still functioning, including life support and security. Looks he took a suit and just... walked away."

"Why didn't you tell me?"

"We did. You didn't respond."

The memory slumped me in my seat. There was one night, a few years back, when I was in a pissy mood and made a drinking game out of watching a bad American romance VR. *Dutchman* had said there was a news alert about Evgeni and I told it to delete it. *Only good news right now.* I suppose part of me had suspected he was gone. "Christ."

"It's just us three now, Mylene. It would be a shame to lose you as well."

And that was Raadhi. She was always the one who remembered birthdays in the lab, who made sure there was food in the kitchen, and who sent cards when there was a death in the family, no matter how distant a relation.

There didn't seem to be much to say after that, so I walked her back to her shuttle. At the airlock, I offered her two open hands, which turned into a silent hug. I held onto her for three long breaths before she stepped away into the connecting tube.

Then I returned to my porthole and watched Raadhi's shuttle drift away from the *Dutchman*. Once she was clear, she fired her main engines and headed back to her animals.

When her drive glare became just another light in the star field, I went to sickbay and checked the medical freezer. It was nominal, as expected. If there had been an actual problem with it, or any system, *Dutchman* would have alerted me.

I just wanted to see it for myself.

In a cylinder surrounded by liquid nitrogen lay a dozen vials of donor sperm that Awusi had edited with her own DNA. It was a surprise gift on our first anniversary. We even went so far as to apply for parent licenses.

But every time I thought about getting pregnant, there was some distraction, some friction between us, some reason not to.

Then came the divorce.

Awusi hadn't asked for the sperm back, so the vials stayed on *Dutchman*. Every now and then I wondered if I should return the cylinder, along with an apology ("Sorry I kept this so long"), but I kept putting it off.

Now I'd lost the chance. The idea of being a parent without her was too depressing.

Then something occurred to me. "*Dutchman*?"

"Here, Mylene."

"Has there been any communication from Awusi's attorney, apart from the... death notice?"

"None."

"What about her trust?"

"It was dissolved according to standard legal protocols. Your name did not appear among the beneficiaries. Would you like a copy?"

I pressed my forehead against the cool bulkhead. Perhaps Awusi *had* forgotten, or didn't care what I did with the sperm. Either way, I thought, I wasn't going to use it.

I lifted my fingers to the control pad and unlocked the door. Alerts flashed in my feed.

"Mylene?" said *Dutchman*. "Do you need assistance?"

I opened cabinets until I found heavy gloves, then opened the freezer. A wave of condensation filled the compartment.

I lifted the cylinder, contemplating. It would be simple enough matter to push the cylinder into a decaying orbit. Or I could cremate it properly with the main engines. That seemed excessive, though.

"Mylene? Do you need assistance?"

"No."

"The medical storage unit is showing rapid temperature increases. Can you confirm?" *Dutchman* was pitching its voice just a tad higher, I noted, trying to show concern without alarming me. That was Awusi's subroutine.

Then I blinked back tears that had nothing to do with the temperature and returned the cylinder to its cradle. I wasn't strong enough to part with her. Not yet. "Everything is fine, *Dutchman*. Continue to monitor the unit."

"Understood."

Did it, really?

As more people joined the Overmind, I found living on Earth less and less attractive. Like many of my generation, I had a harder time adjusting to the forced civic participation and my every utterance monitored for violent or antisocial tendencies. It made the world safer by any measure, but I worried we were losing something fundamental.

Others shared my concern. Off-world emigration exploded. The Overmind eventually caught up, though, imposing its democratic benevolence on the orbital colonies, the moon, and eventually Mars. Diehard libertarians fled into the Oort cloud, where many died when life support systems failed in their private utopias. A lot of people simply starved because they couldn't get enough raw materials for their printers.

When the Overmind began decommissioning the world's remaining military equipment, Awusi and I pooled our then-considerable resources and bought *Dutchman*. The ship was stripped of its weapons, of course, and its AI was cleared of all but basic ship functions, which suited us fine. I took a year to write a new personality matrix while Awusi upgraded *Dutchman*'s living quarters and galley. The armory became a tiny studio. We envisioned ourselves as genteel travelers, hosting salons and intimate dinner parties as we leisurely sailed from Earth-Luna to Mars and back.

But living in such close quarters proved to be too much for us. I loved her, and I know she loved me, yet our disagreements had a very different flavor when you couldn't easily step outside for some air to clear your head. And you never, ever want to put on an e-suit when you're angry.

Not long after Raadhi's visit, I fled Earth orbit at half thrust. As I accelerated beyond Luna, I gave the media avatars the finger by switching off the ship's ansible. It was a stupid gesture and I didn't care. I had faith in *Dutchman*. Now there was nothing to disturb me except fragments of ancient laser messages or whispers calling out on the 21cm band.

Whenever I wanted to get into a really challenging headspace, or explore uncomfortable emotions, I went old school. I turned off my network connection and sat with the work, fighting the temptation to distract myself. Many people considered this a quaint affectation—and maybe it was—though it worked for me.

I figured inspiration came from the flesh. Even a healthy body has to deal with food and drink, discomfort and dreams.

It had been a long time - more than 60 years - since anyone I cared for had died in *veritas*. Each time was a sharp reminder our near-immortality had but one true enemy—despair. For whatever reason, Awusi had unsheathed that cold blade and buried it in her beautiful heart.

She was irrevocably gone, and I couldn't find the words to say how much I loved her.

Some things never changed.

I sailed beyond the home system, setting traps for the elusive Melpomene.

Two months passed in near silence. I found some familiar company in my own presence, in long naps and good books. Then one afternoon the deep radar pinged.

Dutchman reached out its senses. "It appears to be an artificial object."

"Interesting."

I sipped my tea, reviewing the data stream. The radar image was very clear: something was traveling in a straight line, crawling like a human toward a distant mirage of water. If it was a stray rock, someone had given it a push. "Let's go in," I said, securing my cup.

It took thirty minutes for *Dutchman* to match course and speed, putting us a hundred meters away. It was a life pod. This close, there was no doubt. A life pod — in the absolute middle of nowhere.

I wanted to get a closer look, so I loaded up a limited instance of *Dutchman* into a six-armed, general purpose bot, a squid designed for vacuum seas. It jetted over to the life pod, near the airlock, running a tentacle along the machinery like my *grootmoeder* Hendrika checking for dust on the bookcases on cleaning day. God help my brother Johan and I if we missed enough to make a mouse sneeze.

"What do you think?"

"All systems appear dead," reported the bot. "No obvious external damage detected."

The bot sent an image of faded letters stenciled on the skin. *Adiona*, which I presumed was the life pod's mothership. "*Dutchman*, do a search on that name."

The only thing it found in our shipboard database was a brief entry under mythology: *Roman goddess of safe return.* No ship registry, and nothing matching the life pod's design. Likely it was very, very old, built before the Overmind.

I was tempted to switch on the ansible to send a query, but checked the impulse. This was a welcome distraction and I wanted to see how much of this I could figure out before calling home.

"I have new data," the bot said.

"Weapons?" In the old scarcity economies, armed paranoia was the rule of the day.

"None detected. However, scans show one human." A pause. "No life signs."

"Damn. It was a long shot," I said. "Which leave us with essentially an abandoned ship."

"Are you considering salvage?" *Dutchman* asked.

"I don't know. There's definitely something off about it."

"We should be cautious before we do anything too drastic," the ship continued.

"Can you define the technical parameters of 'too drastic'?"

"It's more of an economic question," said Dutchman. "Someone could assert ownership rights and could claim damages against you."

"What is the value of a non-functional machine?" The bot gestured at the ancient tech with a multi-tool.

"You didn't know Roger, my first spouse." Penurious didn't *begin* to describe him." He'd squeeze the tea leaves every morning to make sure he didn't waste *anything*.

"Well," the bot said, "I'd have known that if you'd given me more background information."

"You're pretty cheeky for an AI that didn't exist fifteen minutes ago."

"Yes, ma'am."

"That's better," I said. "Now. Let's bring it onboard."

Before we did, I released a pair of ferrets, small, tenacious AI drones. One headed back along the life pod's line of flight, seeking the pod's mother ship. The other flew forward, swift as an arrow from Diana's bow, to see if we might learn the pod's destination.

The bot rearranged our supplies in the cargo hold to free up more space, then secured the pod inside before returning to its cubby and integrating its memory with the ship. By the time the hold was re-pressurized, I was ready with a maintenance drone and all the tools Dutchman had recommended.

My breath steamed in the cold. The hold would warm eventually, so I set to cutting off rivet heads so I could remove the underlying panel. It was slow going, and my hands began to cramp. I stopped to massage them.

"You don't need to do this," said Dutchman. "My drones can handle it."

"Maybe I don't *need* to do this, but I want to, okay?" I wanted to understand the life pod's *artifice*. It wasn't grown or printed. Even if they had used industrial robots, someone had put the final touches on by hand. I would give it the same respect during its deconstruction.

"My grandfather was an engineer," I said, fitting a power driver to a screw. "He designed the last models of manually controlled vehicles in the Netherlands."

"That must have been interesting."

"He certainly thought so. AI was fairly primitive back then, so his computers were basically dumb databases." I laughed as a long-dormant memory surfaced. "On the day he retired, they let him drive one of the big trucks." Hendrika had always kept a picture from that day, tucked away in a drawer. The entire factory had signed the truck with fluorescent paint pens, turning it into something of an art piece. "I think the company donated it to the Amsterdam Rijksmuseum."

"When you get back, you could look it up."

"Maybe," I said, lifting a bundle of optical fiber. More than likely the building and all its contents had been digitized and recycled long ago.

We worked steadily for another three hours. I narrated and *Dutchman* recorded the disassembly with every sensory we had: optical, auditory, olfactory, and kinesthetic. It might make an interesting teaching module—students could recreate the ancient spacecraft as a school science project, or perhaps the components themselves could be employed as an interactive art exhibit.

That might be its draw: no nano-perfect copies, just the real thing with solid provenance. Something you could actually touch while atonal, contemplative music filled the room. Maybe I could pair a North American cedar flute with a Basque *alboka*. I'd heard one in a café in Madrid and it stuck with me for days—

The cryotube's hatch slid aside under my fingers, revealing a vacuum-desiccated corpse. Judging by the shape of the body and Dutchman's scan of the skeleton, it was a baseline woman, aged 30-35. On the left shoulder was a stylized EU flag. Above the left breast pocket, was the word *Kakra* sewn with gold thread against a black background. "The word doesn't appear anywhere else in the life pod," *Dutchman* noted.

"Probably her name." I searched my ship's library, finding likely candidates in the Twi, Fante, and Akan languages. The name roughly translated as *Twin*. Our guest might be Ghanian, or Ivorian, or a descendant of one of a hundred tribes from that region.

There was no apparent damage to the life pod's interior, and the fuel tanks read empty. Kakra might have launched normally, then exhausted her fuel and coasted. She'd had time to get into the cryotube, trusting the emergency device to keep her in near-stasis for up to five years. I guessed she'd been too far away from rescue. Space is empty in the best of circumstances.

She looked peaceful, lying there. I hoped her last moments weren't filled with shrieking alarms and panic as she injected themself with the sleep drugs.

"Poor thing." *Dutchman*'s digital reconstruction had given her close-cropped frizzy hair, strong cheekbones, long fingers, broad shoulders. I'll bet her smile had lit up the room. Now, she was a mummy. "Sorry we couldn't get to you sooner."

"Now what?" asked *Dutchman*.

"I need something to eat, and some real sleep," I said, suddenly tired. The life pod had appeared toward the end of my day cycle. "We'll continue this in the morning."

"Good night, Mylene."

I returned to my cabin, ate a sandwich, and drank a brandy. I was treading in that uncomfortable space between real fatigue and overtiredness and knew that my brain was useless for any real work. I gave myself permission for a second brandy.

It was probably just grief-influenced memory, but it occurred to me the digital reconstruction could have passed for Awusi.

I scrubbed the tears from my eyes and crawled into bed. In my dreams, I opened the life pod to find the same corpse but it was wearing a lab coat. The name on the badge was *Awusi*.

The Upload Project had an ambitious goal: transfer human conscious into a computational matrix. The invention of biochips—meshes of living memory that could store the Library of Congress a million times over—meant there was space to contain an entire person, all their thoughts and emotions with plenty of room to grow.

It was a wild scheme, funded by obscenely wealthy individuals who feared nothing but death. These modern pharaohs dreamed of living forever, freed of the tyranny of the flesh. Before their bodies fell into eventual decay, they wanted to move their consciousness into indestructible android bodies, or stealthy spacecraft drifting in the asteroid belt.

The early results were disappointing. The initial round of volunteers were drawn from nearby hospices, drawn by generous cash payments and carefully worded contracts that hinted at a possibility of extended life in a virtual environment. The first two volunteers suffered debilitating strokes. Yet another had a fatal heart attack the moment we connected her to the equipment. *Veritas* to *virtu* that were, for all intents and purposes, a functional copy of the original. Those people became the first self-aware Avatars.

"There is good news and bad news," *Dutchman* said while I made breakfast.

"Bad news first," I said, sprinkling powdered sugar on my puffed apple pancake. The meal always reminded me of my favorite diner in Los Angeles, where grads students would cram into booths for cheap breakfasts. Calories and academic arguments.

"While you were sleeping, I was able to fabricate an interface for the life pod's black box."

"Sounds like good news." I poured myself another cup of Raadhi's excellent coffee. I wondered if she were back on Earth, wrestling with some large herbivore. And where was Steven?

"The index is garbage," said Dutchman.

"I guess it would have been too much to ask for. We'll find another way. What's the good news?"

"I can estimate the launch date based on the life pod's last log entry. It's been out there for approximately 175 years, six months."

"That'll shrinks the haystack a bit," I said.

"And there is a system ID - KDanso-Sika."

"Kakra Danso-Sika," I said. "Good to have a name. Next thing is to find out how she died."

Dutchman asked, "Do you wish me to perform an autopsy?"

"I'm sure your drones can handle it better than me."
I had never taken a hands-on biology course.

"The issue is not functionality but legality."

"Oh?" I cut into the pancake. The butter was
printed, but you hardly noticed.

It answered me by posting a summary of a legal
ruling to the nearest display. "The Overmind has no
issue with you taking possession of a derelict
spacecraft—"

"Life pod."

"—or any similar artifact, provided you submit the
appropriate paperwork and pay reclamation fees. The
disposition of Danso-Sika is another matter entirely." It
highlighted the date of the ruling. "Even though the
corpse in our possession died before the Human
Remains Act became law, it is retroactive. We cannot
take any actions that may 'violate the religious
traditions, if any' of said corpse."

"But we have no idea what she believed, if
anything. She could have been a Wiccan for all we
know."

"That's beside the point," said *Dutchman*. "Until we
determine her beliefs, we cannot perform any
destructive tests on her."

"Well, shit." I nibbled on a soya patty. "I guess we'll
have to settle for a deep scan."

"My medical systems *are* quite sophisticated," it
said.

"Well, get on with it," I grumbled, and returned to
my breakfast.

Dutchman dispatched two drones. They moved
Kakra's body into sickbay, cut away her shipsuit, and

placed her onto the examination table. Medical sensors emerged from the bulkhead and began scanning.

I cleaned up and went to sickbay with my second cup of coffee. Going through the shipsuit, nearby, I found an empty drug injector, a dried-out, brittle plastic pen and a piece of paper with some faded writing. *Dutchman*'s gas chromatograph showed only traces of the expected metabolic depressants in the injector. I ran an image of the paper through a translator.

The best estimate was formal Akan: *I was born with her, and I wanted to die with her.*

Part of a poem, maybe? Dialog from her favorite movie?

My display pinged. The deep scan showed no signs of long-term illness or recent physical injuries. There was an very old, cleanly healed break on her right humerus. Maybe she had been an active child, climbing trees or skating on concrete. "Based on the information we have," *Dutchman* said, "the probability is she died by asphyxiation."

That made sense. Even in coldsleep, her cells needed *some* oxygen.

"There is something else." *Dutchman* pointed out a biochip interface at the base of her occiput. Curious and curiouser: an interface officer.

There was a very brief window—perhaps twenty years—when commercial and military ships had carried interface officers. Eventually, AI systems became sophisticated enough to handle ship functions without direct neural connections, and those risky surgeries fell out of favor.

Further investigation turned up tendrils of nanofiber connecting the biochip with her frontal cortex. It was very similar to the Overmind mesh injected into every citizen before adolescence. "Whoever put this into her was working with bleeding edge tech, which means we might be able to track down the manufacturer." Now I really wished we could excise the nanofibers and subject them to a proper scrutiny. Unfortunately, it was out of the question. "I guess we've done everything we can for the moment. Go ahead and put the body into cold storage," I said. "Once we figure out if she had a spiritual practice, we can figure out what to do with her. With respect, of course."

"Of course, Mylene."

I stretched and heard my back crack. "Ouch."

"Maybe you should exercise."

"You know, you're sounding more like my *grootmoeder* Hendrika all the time."

"I'll take that as a compliment."

Dutchman wasn't wrong; I needed to move. The ship's central section normally spun to provide 0.99g of pseudo gravity, but all it meant was I was getting the equivalent exercise of sitting in a chair on Earth. To keep ahead of bone density loss, I had to *do* something. So I warmed up with some stretches, then ran on the treadmill for an hour, pushing myself to the beat of late twentieth-first century dance remixes. Awusi couldn't stand them, but I found them wonderfully distracting. After the treadmill, I switched to the resistance bands and starting working my upper body.

"The ferrets have reported in," Dutchman announced as I finished my first set. "Unit 1 deployed telescopes but found nothing within the life pod's estimated flight path." The mirror next to me switched over to a navigation chart. A red line projected forward from our current position, and a blue line trailed behind. "There is no human settlement within range."

"So Kakra was just going... nowhere?"

"So it would seem."

"What about the launch point?"

"Unit 2 made estimates but there are many variables," Dutchman replied. "Time of departure, initial fuel supply—"

"I think we can assume the life pod left shortly after Kakra accessed it. I would also assume the life pod was fully fueled."

"We still don't know the engine burn profile."

I considered that. "Maybe we can extrapolate something from known spacecraft of the period. Meanwhile, let's see if we can find *Adiona*. Set a course for..." I pointed at the blue line. "There."

"I can do so, Mylene, but please consider our own consumables."

"I don't mind eating rations." I wasn't thrilled with the idea, but as long as the coffee and the booze held out, I could manage.

"The life pod coasted for 175 years. That's a lot of space to cover."

"Well, *we* won't be coasting," I said. It was a pretty feeble argument.

"Correct," said *Dutchman*. "We'll be burning our own fuel reserves on a course that takes us away from

Earth. We will eventually reach a point where we don't have enough fuel to return in comfort."

"I don't have any pressing engagements."

"You'd have to spend the return journey in an emergency cryotube if we get too far from inhabited space."

The prospect didn't please me. "Steven would never let me live *that* down." I unwrapped a protein bar, suddenly hungry. "Still, I'd like to see what we can find."

"I would advise against that, Mylene."

"I'm sure it'll be fine."

"I am confident in my own skills and the state of the ship. But there is another consideration here." A dense block of text appeared on my display. "The Recovery and Reunification statues are very clear when it comes to human remains."

"Those were written to deal with natural disasters and armed conflict," I said. "They don't specifically apply in this case."

"Some legal software might disagree with your position."

"Let's say you're correct. What do you suggest, *Dutchman*?"

"Setting aside Danso-Sika's remains, you are bound by law to file a discovery notice."

I snorted. "The *Adiona* is *long* overdue. I sincerely doubt anyone is waiting for news at this point."

"The law still applies. You must file the notice."

"Well, I'll think about it," I said, and went to my piano.

Brahms is perfect music for frustration. It's easy to lose yourself in it; just claw your way through those chords and set your teeth to buzzing. As a child, I'd been a difficult music student. I had talent, like my mother, but I lacked her passion. There were always more interesting things to do than practice, like read or ride my bike or code. But my *grootmoeder* made it clear if I were going to live in her house, I would learn to play an instrument like a civilized person. So I did.

My music never earned me a scholarship, or helped me find a date. It did, however, give me a refuge. When my parents went to prison for hacking into an offshore drilling platform, my *grootmoeder* Hendrika was awarded custody of my brother Johan and I.

She kept me at the keyboard two hours a day longer than my teacher required. After Hendrika died, I practically lived in the rehearsal studio. It was more useful than the grief counseling offered by government.

Eventually, all that practice—coupled with my celebrity as a First Uploader—led to a second career. I never played any grand old venues but I had a loyal, if select, fan base.

For my wedding present, Awusi tracked down my *grootmoeder*'s Steinway and had it installed in our flat in Lyon. Eventually it moved with us to *Dutchman*.

I suspect it's the largest classical instrument to travel beyond the Kuiper Belt.

Once I'd dealt with Herr Brahms, I sponged off and dressed in clean clothes. Then I made a fresh pot of tea and sat down in my office, calling up new virtual workspaces. One corner was dedicated to a real-time display of *Dutchman's* systems. Everything showed green, save the ansible, which was still in yellow standby mode.

Part of me really wanted to sit out here and unravel this mystery at my own pace. I could feel my brain starting to engage again, and it was a welcome respite from the fog of grief. But there was another part of me that absolutely felt Hendrika's disapproval at the very *thought* of ignoring the law.

With a sigh, I woke up the ansible and submitted queries to the Overmind. While *Dutchman* compiled results, I checked my personal message queue. My filters had scorched everything except a note from Raadhi and a photo from Steven with the subject line *Honeymoon*.

It showed Steven atop the pyramid at the Temple of Kulkan at Chichén Itzá, flanked by a man and a woman whom I gathered were his new spouses. They radiated confidence and joy. Or maybe it was the sunburn and the gorgeous sunrise backlighting the scene.

I'll admit I was jealous.

When I expanded the image, I could just make out a jaguar at the edge of the tree line. I wondered if one of Raadhi's teams had worked on that project.

I turned to Raadhi's note. She had analyzed Awusi's movements for the last six months of her life and conducted interviews with as many people on her contact list as she could. She'd even interrogated her literary estate AI, which offered several other avenues of investigation.

None of them panned out. At this point, everything pointed to the same conclusion.

Awusi was truly gone.

I was a little surprised how much of me still clung to the hope she might have faked her own death. I counted a few long breaths and brought myself back to the task at hand, despite the ache in my chest. That's what Hendrika would do.

Dutchman displayed the first two thousand hits from my query. Nothing on the *Adiona* itself, although there were matches between several components in the life pod and a factory catalog from the correct time period. I took thirty minutes to create a non-profit foundation to research the life pod, declaring myself its caretaker. The Overmind chewed this over for an hour, then granted me temporary custody, pending final review. It also ordered me to make "reasonable" efforts to "safeguard and return" Kakra's remains.

"It's probably for the best."

"Oh? I thought you wanted to hold on to the remains."

"I did," I said. "Then I realized I might be dealing with some of my own issues here. Like Johan." His body was never recovered from the mountains. The funeral had felt so empty.

"Yes, Mylene, it's probably best we reunite Kakra with her family."

I tapped my index finger against the display. "Can you plot a fast return course given our fuel?"

"Without a doubt, Mylene."

"Then take us back to terra firma, *Dutchman*."

The engines came online, and my sense of gravity shifted as *Dutchman* adjusted the module's spin. Once my inner ear settled, I opened a design file for an unfinished stage set. I raised the rear facade and added an outline of Monte Perdido. That led me to a musical score, a *thème de la déconstruction,* if you will. I lifted the bones of it from Debussy's *Première rhapsodies* but the muscles and skin were my own. I wanted something to represent the *Adiona,* but lacked any real sense of the ship. How big was it? How many crew? I must have been fiddling around for some time, because I was interrupted by a drone bearing a tray. I opened the cover to find rice, tofu, root vegetables, and yellow curry.

"Thank you, *Dutchman,*" I said.

"Bon appetite."

I closed out my workspace while I ate. It was an old habit, courtesy of Hendrika, who insisted we leave our books and screens in the other room during meals. It used to bother me, especially during my teen years, but later I learned to appreciate the simple act of doing one thing at a time. The work would always be there when you put down your fork.

After finishing the excellent curry, I poured over *Dutchman's* research but still didn't see anything that definitively tied the *Adiona* and Kakra together.

"This is frustrating."

"You've only just started," *Dutchman* said. "Call it a night."

I was about to say I wasn't tired, but then a yawn seized me. "All right."

"Good night, Mylene. I'll wake you if something important happens."

"I would expect nothing less."

I had a bad dream that night. I was floating in vacuum, and *Dutchman* was speeding away, ignoring my panicked cries for help. Hendrika's voice on the radio admonished me for not checking my safety line.

It took me two days to review everything the Overmind had sent us. I suppose I could have written some research protocols to move things along faster, but that sort of programming was never my strong suit. I guess I was hoping for something obvious, or some intuition to kick in.

I had the drones pull DNA from the Kakra's suit. We didn't get a match any closer than a common ancestor five generations back. On the other hand, *Dutchman's* digital reconstruction generated a lot of hits on available image archives. Too many, as it turned out. Plenty of people looked *like* her, but none of the images were Kakra. *Dutchman* also scoured thousands of social media postings, looking for clues.

And all of this ansible time was burning through my dwindling credit.

A week later, I was stuck.

"It doesn't appear you've missed anything," said *Dutchman*. "From what I can see, the Overmind doesn't have information directly linking Danso-Sika to the *Adiona*."

"I don't understand. Are there that many people named Kakra Danso-Sika?" I said. "That was a rhetorical question by the way."

"Try not to be so hard on yourself, Mylene. It's very possible she left behind an extensive life record. We may simply be unable to access it. The consolidation conflicts were expensive in both lives and data."

I remembered. Entire government archives vanished almost overnight, sometimes by their own hand, in a last-ditch effort to purge their history before joining the Overmind. Somewhere in the process, Kakra had apparently disappeared along with millions of others.

"We could turn our attention to offline archives," continued Dutchman. "Data archeologists and hobbyists are constantly adding new information to the Overmind's databases."

"That doesn't help me now." I hated the petulant tone in my voice.

"You could hire human agents and expand your search. But that may not be prudent given your finances."

"Oh?" I checked my account. "Oh dear." I had dropped below one million credits for the first time since the Overmind took over. That would barely cover a full resupply of the ship. "Something's not right."

"The Overmind voted in a new consumption tax."

"Shit." *Dutchman* was one of a handful of private spacecraft still in existence, and I suspected the Overmind permitted me this exemption because of my status as a First Uploader. But I still had to pay for upkeep.

If my credit dropped much further, I'd have to sign on to a big public service project or organize a performance tour just to keep the lights on. Awusi's memorial might bring in a few credits, but I didn't want to "monetize my humanity," as my father used to say. I squeezed my eyes shut and took several calming breaths against the rising acid in my stomach. "I could use a hand here. Any ideas?"

"Ask for volunteers. There are still plenty of discrete people in *veritas* who might want to help."

"All right," I said. "Make the arrangements." As much as I hated to admit it was clear I needed extra hands.

"I'll do that, Mylene."

"Thank you."

I indulged in a bath, transferring Kakra's note into a front pocket of my robe like some kind of talisman. *I was born with her, and I wanted to die with her.*

It was something Awusi might have written.

My legally necessary foundation transformed into a physical operation, with a tiny office in Rotterdam that had once housed a tobacco and sweet shop. *Dutchman* contacted universities, museums, and private researchers, dangling bits of our findings to see who nibbled. Over the course of a week we vetted forty-eight volunteers throughout Europe and Africa and directed them to focus on the years when interface surgeries were still in vogue.

The first real break came when an optical scan of the pod's interior turned up parts of an inspection sticker inside a maintenance panel. The sticker was signed by Luca Moretti, an employee of the defunct Argotec Space, S.A. One researcher was able to locate restaurant reviews attributed to Moretti, and used corresponding marketing data to track down his personal blog from an archive of decommissioned web servers. I read his blog while putting in my treadmill time.

Moretti had written an article for a trade journal describing his work on the *Adiona*'s life pods. He'd also inspected the life pods on the *Khonsu*, which Argotec Space had completed thirteen months earlier.

"*Khonsu* is the Egyptian god of the moon," *Dutchman* commented after it scanned the blog. "He was known as a traveler or wanderer, depending on the translation."

Moretti noted that the *Adiona* returned six weeks ahead of schedule, minus her Interface Officer, but didn't comment further due to pending legal action against the company.

"Any information on the lawsuit, *Dutchman*?"

"The first ship, *Khonsu*, was lost with all hands on her maiden voyage due to a fusion drive malfunction," *Dutchman* said. "There are corroborating news stories in trusted archives. The families of the crew pursued legal recourse through EU courts, citing common safety standards for atmospheric craft."

"Interesting approach." Commercial space travel wasn't exactly common at the time. "Let's see if we can get anything from the court records."

Fortunately, those still existed, although someone had to scan physical copies and upload them. They arrived two days later, and I read them while eating a faux meat pie with one hand and scribbling notes with the other. One of Dutchman's drones quietly collected crumbs from the deck.

Thirty-eight separate lawsuits against Argotec eventually morphed into a class-action case, which the company settled minutes before their first scheduled hearing. Simultaneously, Argotec filed for bankruptcy with an eye toward reconstituting themselves under new management. The company's investors decided to cut their losses, though, and sell off the IP and manufacturing facilities to Virgin Intergalactic. Moretti lost his job along with most of the original Argotec Space employees.

When I dug deeper into the bankruptcy filing, I found worker compensation payouts, including death benefits paid to the family of *Adiona's* interface officer: *Kakra Danso-Sika*. Her employee ID showed a woman with large, dark eyes who did not smile for the camera.

Dutchman declared its digital reconstruction of our passenger wasa 91 percent match for the photo.

"Pleased to meet you, Danso-Sika," I said. "Although I think after all this time we should be on a first-name basis." I yawned and went to the galley for a cup of coffee. As I poured the water into the press, I had a thought. "*Dutchman!*"

"Yes, Mylene?" I stirred in sugar using a maple wood spoon Awusi had purchased in an open air market in Madrid. I used to have a whole collection of handmade kitchen tools before the divorce.

"Were there any other deaths on the *Adiona*?"

"No. The ship returned to orbit with 36 out of 37 crew members."

"And it didn't launch a second mission?"

"Correct. The company was dissolved before the *Adiona* was refitted."

Two missions: one a catastrophic failure and one aborted due to a crew death. No wonder Argotec's investors had abandoned them.

But something kept nagging me. I took my coffee bulb back to my desk and re-read Kakra's file. There was no formal autopsy, only an affidavit from the ship's medical officer stating Kakra had died as result of a cerebral hemorrhage, and her body was "interred" in space using the life pod as a "burial container."

That was a lie.

She was *alive* when she'd launched the life pod and written her cryptic note.

"*Dutchman*, can you estimate the cost of the life pod?"

Since it now had access to Argotec's manufacturing records, the answer didn't take long. "Ten million, six hundred thousand Euros at the time of manufacture. Approximately value 12,000,000 Euros at the time the Overmind froze all currency."

Back in those days, twenty Euros bought a loaf of bread or a bouquet of flowers. Twelve million Euros was *real* money. Surely the captain wouldn't have allowed his crew to throw away something so expensive—not to mention mission critical—when a biohazard bag would have served.

So I played out a possible scenario: Kakra had launched the life pod when the ship wasn't in any danger. The *Adonia*'s safe return was certainly evidence of that. And as the Interface Officer, Kakra had direct control of the ship's systems. It would have been possible to lock out the rest of the crew before she launched. By the time they regained control of the ship, she was too far away to retrieve, and the captain had falsified his logs to cover the theft.

Even if that scenario were true, one glaring question remained: *Why had she abandoned ship?*

I prowled the length of *Dutchman*, the caffeine warring with my fatigue. I came across a drones misting one of the climbing vines that lined the corridor and patted its carapace.

When I reached the junction for sickbay, I turned in that direction, coming to a stop in front of the cylinder where we had stored Kakra. I took her note from my pocket.

I was born with her and I wanted to die with her.

I was born with her—

Then it clicked.

"*Dutchman*, pull up the wrongful death claims payments settled by Argotec. Can you list the recipients?"

"Here are the payment schedules, alpha sort by last name." Dutchman flashed them to the display nearest me. I scanned the list until I found *two* payments to M/M Danso-Sika:

--Death - Accidental: Child/Dependent, Kakra Danso-Sika, Interface Officer. Assignment: ship operations (*Adiona*)

--Death - Accidental: Child/Dependent, Ataá Pánin Danso-Sika, Interface Officer. Assignment: ship operations (*Khonsu*)

When I highlighted the second name and asked for a translation, it came back as "Younger twin."

Twin. My heart raced.

Kakra had a twin sister: *Ataá Pánin,* who had died with all hands aboard the *Khonsu.* Two years later or thereabouts, Kakra had launched her life pod into the void. I was sure of it.

When I was eight years old, my brother and I had begged our parents for a dog. But Johan and I competed with each other in everything, and never wanted to share. Our father was legitimately worried that if he brought a dog into the house, it might become another point of contention between us. He refused.

We continued our efforts, forming a temporary alliance for this one battle.

After many tense dinners, Father announced he would get us a dog *if* we kept up our grades and *if* did *all* our chores promptly and without complaint.

In the subsequent months, we weeded the garden and washed the dishes, practiced our instruments, and earned prizes at the school science fair. Johan, a year my senior, threatened terrible retribution if I failed to hold up my end. I swore to watch him like a falcon and report the slightest infraction to Mama.

It was a long summer.

A few weeks before school started up again, our father called Johan and I into the backyard. He opened the toolshed and retrieved a crate, which contained not one but *two* Border Collie puppies. From the same litter.

"They're exactly alike in every way." And then he had grinned, thinking he had sabotaged any complaint one or the other sibling had gotten the "better" pet.

In that moment, we didn't care. It was a brilliant Sunday morning and we rolled around the grass, being licked by two bundles of furry exuberance.

"Mylene, are you all right?"

I sniffled. "Fine. Just thinking about my brother."

"I see," said Dutchman. "Can I help?"

Even though I knew I'd programmed the response, it still made me laugh. "Start up a new Overmind search. Find out everything you can about Ataá Pánin. Maybe she'll lead us to her sister."

I returned the note to my pocket and took myself to bed, where I feel asleep reading *The Wind in the Willows*. It was one of Johan's favorite books.

I dreamed of running through a forest, flanked by two Border Collies. Johan was nowhere to be seen.

I woke and followed my nose to the gallery, where coffee and fresh oatmeal, a strawberry compote, and smoked fish awaited.

"Well, this is lovely. What's the occasion?"

"National Smoked Fish Day in Canada."

"Really?"

Dutchman paused a moment before answering. "According to my database, today is International Customs Day in America, Festival of Sheep Shearing in Scotland, Feast of St. Ignatius, and Ice Cream Appreciation Day in Brazil."

"I'm glad you left off the ice cream." I spooned compote into my oatmeal.

"You're welcome," said *Dutchman*. "I was trying to engage you with food and conversation since I have received information that may be difficult to hear. You may recall the incident with Evgeni."

I winced. "Point taken. What's the news?"

"A salvage firm has challenged your claim to the life pod under the terms of a contract that shows a direct inheritance of assets traced back to Argotec's bankruptcy. The Overmind has issued a temporary injunction against you pending a final ruling."

"In other words, I can't touch it."

"That would be best," said *Dutchman*.

Fortunately, I didn't need physical access to the life pod right now. "Well, I suppose you should go ahead and seal everything up." Once the drones had wrapped the life pod's components in artificial spider silk, we could store it indefinitely. "What about Ataá Panin?"

"Better news. One of your volunteers found a news archive about a set of twin students in Ghana who graduated with engineering degrees. The women had attended university on scholarships funded by several commercial space companies, one of which was Argotec SA."

"So we know who she is."

"It's not absolute, though confidence is high."

"We need to be sure," I said. "Are there genetic records for either sister available?"

"No. There are, however, living relatives."

"Well, what are you waiting for? Let's go talk to them."

"Yes, Mylene. You have time to finish your breakfast before I adjust our burn."

"Much appreciated." I reached for the smoked fish.

Apart from direct transfer of a human consciousness into *virtu*, Project Upload was also trying to devise ways to make non-destructive recordings. The idea was to have, in the words of the business plan, "the ultimate personal backup." Everything you knew could be saved on a regular basis, and then uploaded in the event of an emergency.

It took eight months—and buying out another startup for their biochip patents—but in the end we found a way to copy and store someone's life in a substrate of superdense memory. The volunteers reported minor headaches during the recording and loss of balance after, both of which disappeared in less than an hour.

Of course, almost everyone found an excuse to make a "personal" recording after hours. Everything was fine, until we hooked Awusi up to the scanner.

She'd avoided alcohol and eaten a light meal, following the established protocols. About thirty minutes into the scan, she slipped into a light REM sleep. But then her blood pressure and heart rate began to rise. She struggled awake and she wept for ten straight minutes, until she ran out of tears and snot and lay there gasping for breath.

Then she fell into a hard, deep sleep. We cleaned her up and waited an hour, then another. She didn't stir. Finally, I set a watch and encouraged the rest of the team to get back to work. There was data to collate and reports to write.

Awusi moaned in her sleep and occasionally twitched.

At four am, during my shift, her eyes flew open. She seized my hand.

"I've seen the goddess, Mylene."

"Hey, hey, it's all right," I said. "You're fine." I pulled out my phone with my free hand. "Let me tell Dr. Ruiz you're awake." Our neurologist had left orders to call her when Awusi regained consciousness.

"Not yet," Awusi said. "Give me a minute. Please."

"Sure." I glanced at the display above the bed. None of the indicators showed red. If there were a real problem, I could hit the panic button and summon a crash team. I squeezed her hand. "Are you thirsty? Hungry?" The experiment had started sixteen hours before.

"Thirsty."

I gave her a bottle of electrolyte solution, which she drank very slowly. Later, she would write in her autobiography that she'd always disliked the chemical aftertaste of electrolytes, but on this occasion, all the flavors—even the artificial grape—"danced on her tongue."

"So..." I said after she drained the bottle. "Tell me about this goddess."

"She was huge and dark-skinned and beautiful and all I wanted was to wrap my arms around her." She looked wistful.

"Sounds nice."

"It seemed so real," she said. "She smelled of cinnamon and vanilla... and onions simmering in hot oil. There were plants everywhere, like a nursery, you know? But we were outside. And there was a warm breeze..."

"People have reported some weird shit when we hooked them into the neural network."

"Maybe," she said, rolling the empty bottle between her hands. "It felt real, though. All of it."

"You want another one?"

She nodded. I gave her the cherry flavor and called the neurologist.

Once we entered orbit, *Dutchman* gave me a number for an office in London. The man who answered my call appeared physically young, but projected confidence beyond his apparent years. I guessed he was on his second body.

"M. Kwame Danso-Sika? This is Mylene Vandenberg calling."

"Good morning, M. Vandenberg. This is a great honor." He bobbed his head and smiled. I could see Kakra's DNA written in his jawline.

"Please, I'm far too old for flattery." I waved my hands. "Call me Mylene."

"And you must call me Kwame. I am a great fan of your photography. And your *other* work, of course." He winked. Damn, he was handsome. "Now, what can I do you for today?"

I took a deep breath and released it. *Dutchman* was 99% sure but still.... "I wish to ask you a question. Two questions, really."

Kwame leaned back in his chair. Sunlight from a nearby window played on his tight black curls. "Please continue."

"Is—was—your grandfather Táwia Danso-Sika? I'm sorry if I'm not getting the pronunciation right."

"Your pronunciation is fine. And yes, my grandfather is Táwia, but I imagine your AI already told you that."

"It never hurts to verify things," I said. "And your grandfather had two sisters?"

"Yes, twins."

Here goes. Below the range of the camera, I clenched my hands together. "I have recently returned from beyond the Charon's orbit..." *While trying to deal with my ex-wife's suicide.* "Well... I stumbled across a life pod belonging to the deep spacecraft *Adiona*. It contained the remains of Kakra Danso-Sika. At least, I think it's her."

Kwame's eyes widened. "Ghost stories an hour after breakfast. Well, I'm definitely going to need another cup of coffee." He flicked his fingers on a virtual terminal. "How did you find such a thing?"

"Pure chance." I gave him an abbreviated version of events. "If you're interested, I can send you my nav logs."

His coffee arrived, borne on a silver office bot. There was also a small pitcher of milk or cream. I made a mental note to send him some of Raadhi's beans. Kwame mixed his coffee with a small spoon, his movements slow and precise. As he set the spoon aside I saw his hands betray a tremor.

After he'd taken a healthy swallow, he called up his virtual keyboard again. "I presume you'll want my DNA records for a comparison with the... remains."

I nodded. "If you don't mind." Normally, I would have made a request through the Overmind, but this warranted a personal call.

"I have sent you a secure link."

Dutchman pinged my display. *Handshake established. Comparing datasets now.* By the time Kwame took another sip, we had an answer. "It's a match," I said.

He set his cup down and clapped his hands once. "Well! This is turning out to be a most extraordinary day. I'll leave the office early so I can begin planning the funeral."

"I'm sorry to bring you such bad news," I said.

"Oh, no!" He laughed and wiped away a tear. "This is a *happy* day for me." He told me he was the last male of his family line still living on Earth. "It will be a perfect occasion to bring some cousins home. Kakra was a very important member of the clan. Her funeral and life celebration will be special indeed." He laughed again. "You will come, I hope."

"I'd be honored," I said.

"We look forward to having you." He pursed his lips. "This is going to upset our vacation plans, but I think my husband will forgive me."

Awusi used to talk about attending funerals when she was a child, and how they frequently cost more than weddings. "If you need help with the expenses, I can donate some credits."

"Thank you, Mylene, but I must refuse. You have done more than enough," he said. "Besides, there will be no shortage of contributions, I think, once I announce the who the funeral is celebrating. Kakra! Strange and wonderful times, indeed."

"Then I'll let you get on with it. *Dutchman* can coordinate with your system for the particulars," I said. "Thank you again for your time."

"No, thank *you*, Mylene. I'm in your debt." He closed the connection.

I leaned back and blew out a long breath. My knot in my stomach began untying itself. "*Dutchman*?"

"Getting contact information now," it said. "His system calls itself *Wowa*. It has a lovely accent."

"I'm pleased. Let me know when they set a firm date." I glanced at the image of Earth spinning in my display.

I was going home.

I was drafting the audio script for the life pod exhibit when *Dutchman* interrupted. "You have a message."

"I'm really busy. Are they on my approved list?"

"No, Mylene."

"Then shunt it into the queue, please." The Overmind had recently ruled in my favor, awarding me full custody of the life pod, so I was anxious to finalize my designs. The preliminary bids on my proposal gave me hope the eventual profits would keep *Dutchman* running a long time.

"The caller's credentials were sufficiently interesting I thought your communications filter might be flexible on this occasion. Her name is Efia Danso-Sika."

"A relation?"

"A cousin," replied Dutchman. "And she is most anxious to speak with you."

"Okay, call her back."

"The message says she would prefer to talk in person, and that she's willing to make the trip from her home in Armstrong City."

I looked it up. Armstrong City was a retirement community perched on the edge of Tycho crater. "Pretty close." While I didn't want to be around people just yet, I'd be interacting with large numbers soon enough. Might as well dip my toe in the water. "Go ahead and order her a shuttle. My treat."

I went to find something presentable to wear.

Efia Danso-Sika was a wrinkled, hunched woman who looked like she might mass all of 40 kilos. Her head was bald save for a few wisps of white hair. At her request, I reduced the spin of the main module so our gravity was closer to Luna standard. Even that seemed to tax her.

"I'm not going to the funeral because I'm too damn old," she announced after I'd settled her in a lounger. "I can't stand the gravity, and I don't want to move into a clone." She flexed one liver-spotted hand. "It wouldn't be me."

"I understand."

"Do you now?" Efia said. "I've read about you. There was a time when you had the sense to look your age; not now. You could pass for one of my granddaughters."

I let the remark pass. "What did you want to talk about?"

The old woman craned her neck toward the porthole. "No privacy down here." She tapped her forehead with her thumb. "No privacy *up here*."

"I doubt the Overmind monitors off-world retirement homes very closely."

"You can't be too careful," said Efia. "To be honest, I'd almost forgotten about the *Khonsu* until I got the invitation to the funeral."

"You mean Kakra's ship, the *Adiona*."

"*No*, I mean the *Khonsu*. The one that blew up." She sighed. "You got anything to drink around here?"

Once Efia had a bulb of brandy cradled in both hands, she continued her story. "I know I signed the agreement and took their money, but that was a long time ago and everyone involved is dead. Well, almost everyone." She chuckled.

"It was such a huge deal when Argotec recruited the girls right out of school. They were barely 18 and didn't know anything about anything," she said. "Despite some disagreement about letting them go to Europe, the signing bonus was enough to pay off their parent's house, and buy tailored meds for some auntie's cancer. So that was that."

"Real corporate money," I said.

"You said it," she said. "The girls were healthy and had top marks in mathematics. Best candidates, they said. What they didn't say—and what we figured out later—was they wanted to see how their interface worked on identical twins."

I nodded. First-generation nanotech was unpredictable, to say the least. Identical twins meant one less variable in the trial.

"The girls went away for training and sent us nice letters and silly gifts. And when they turned 25, Argotec named Ataá Pánin as their first Interface Officer, and Kakra as the backup. Everyone was so proud."

I repeated her words. "And then the *Khonsu* blew up."

She sipped her brandy. "They put the whole program on hold after that. Paid Kakra's contract and sent her home. Not that it made any difference."

"What do you mean?"

Efia shook her head. "She was a ghost, that girl. Oh, she ate and slept, and she even got herself a job teaching calculus, but she was a ghost."

The silence grew awkward. Then I spoke up, surprising myself, "When I was about her age, my brother Johan died in a mountain climbing accident. We were close. Very close." I could still recall his sunburned face as he drove off that morning. "It was like losing part of myself. I can only imagine how difficult it would have been for Kakra, losing a twin."

The old woman's eyes softened. "It was terrible. Everyone thought Kakra was going to fade away completely, but she surprised them. One day, the story goes, she showed up at breakfast and said she was going to finish what she started. She started emailing and calling Argotec, doing interviews with the media, putting pressure on the company to restart the program. About two years later they launched the *Adiona*."

"And she didn't come back," I said.

"Until now, M. Vandenberg. Until now." She leaned forward and put a hand on my arm. "Do you think I might see her?"

"Of course."

We walked with painful slowness down to sickbay. I had Efia wait in the passageway while I dimmed the lights and arranged a blanket over the corpse. Then I called her in. She pulled back the blanket and laid her fingertips gently to her cousin's forehead. Then she whispered, "*Asase Yaa* will take care of you now, child," and drew the blanket up.

"I should be getting back," she said. "I'm sure you have a million things to do."

We walked slowly back to the airlock. Efia leaned on me, despite the low *g*. "Have you ever been to a Ghanian funeral?"

"No."

"They are something special. You married a Ghanian woman, didn't you?"

I nodded. "We got divorced. There was a part of her I couldn't understand, couldn't connect with."

Efia's smile was equal parts memory and empathy. "Even if people love each other until the stars fall out of the sky, they can't really know each other. My husband JoJo was like that. He's been dead twenty years now. No, twenty-one, that's right.

"Before I came to the moon I went through everything in storage, oh, boxes and disks and heaven knows what else. And I found his journal."

"What did you learn?" I asked.

"Didn't read it," she said. "I recycled it."

I was confused. "Weren't you curious?"

"Of course I was!" Her voice cracked. "*And* those were his private thoughts. If he wanted me to know them, he would have told me. I needed to respect that."

She climbed into her shuttle.

It took four weeks to organize everything. Some of Kwame's family were in long-term medical facilities, hesitant to make the journey home. Others needed to wait on clones so they could attend the event in younger bodies. *Everyone* sent sympathy notes and flowers. *Wowa* forwarded an image of a living room filled with so many flowers (real and holographic) there was barely room for Kwame and a red-haired man I took to be the aforementioned husband, Harry.

Kwame grinned like a child on his birthday.

I took advantage of the delay to get in touch with Steven. He was too busy to visit, though he promised we'd get together in Paris for New Year's Eve. "With Raadhi, of course. You should call her."

"This is so embarrassing," I said when she picked up. "I *completely* forgot it was December."

"You've had other things on your mind," she said. "I'm sure *Dutchman* would have reminded you if you'd left instructions."

"I suppose." Even though Awusi and I hadn't celebrated Christmas together in decades, she always sent a little something. I made a point to drink a toast to her, usually from an open community party in Rotterdam. I liked to immerse myself in familiar accents and stuff myself with chocolate and marzipan on Christmas Eve.

I missed the bonfires. The Overmind restricted us to portable heaters and holograms.

"Next year will be different," I said. "I'm going to start my own tradition and throw a ridiculous holiday dinner and invite all the neighbors over. Spend three days cooking and another one cleaning up, just like Hendrika used to."

"It will be a pretty small party if you're still living up there."

"You never know, Raadhi. I might be looking for a new place soon."

"Oh?" She cocked her head to one side.

"I've been thinking about what you said. About retirement."

"*Good.* Where?"

"I'm still working on that part."

"Don't forget to leave a forwarding address so I can send you coffee."

"Could you send me a box now? I'd like to bring some to the funeral."

"Is that a traditional gift?" she said.

"I have no idea," I said, "although Kwame looked like someone who enjoys a cup."

"In that case, I'll make up a special blend."

"Thank you."

"It's really no bother," Raadhi said. "See you soon."

Dutchman filed a flight plan and synched the shuttle's nav system to Overmind traffic control. My own pilot training was limited to emergency procedures, which meant following checklists and staying out *Dutchman*'s way. There was no way I was going to fly us in.

On my last trip home, I'd come down with as little fanfare as possible. This time, I allowed the media drones to broadcast my flight as I departed *Dutchman*, made a few leisurely orbits, then dropped toward Africa. The shuttle shook a bit on re-entry but I'd experienced worse turbulence in commercial aircraft over the English Channel.

I hugged the Prime Meridian from France to Ghana, slowly shedding velocity until my final slow turns over Kumasi. My hosts had asked to meet me at the old regional airport there, which now served as a cargo terminal for trans atmospheric traffic. After the shuttle rolled to a stop, I activated my temporary Overmind link, shrugged off my harness and tried to smooth the wrinkles from my dress. I had decided to forego my formal black suit, and instead wore an outfit *Dutchman* had printed out the night before. The dress mimicked kente cloth, with short sleeves, a tight waist and flared hips. I bound my hair in a bright silk scarf Awusi had given me when I met her family for the first time.

I felt awkward. However, *Dutchman* had received a protocol package from *Wowa*, and assured me my outfit was appropriate for the occasion.

Unlike my previous visit, I was allowing incoming messages. *Dutchman* had posted teasers of my work on Kakra's life pod, and media traffic was ramping up. I flagged a number of interview requests for later. Right now, I needed to deal with people in the flesh.

It was easy to pick Kwame and Harry from the crowd. They wore colorful matching jackets and red kerchiefs. Behind them waited a dozen young women carrying armloads of flowers. Kwame strode onto the ancient tarmac, hands outstretched. He met me on the ramp and shook both my hands vigorously.

"Welcome home, Mylene!"

"Home is a little town called Bredeweg, in the Netherlands," I said.

He released my hands and gestured around him. "I myself was born not far from here. Nonetheless, we are both children of Earth. So again I say, welcome home!"

"I concede the point."

"I can see we will be great friends, Mylene. Now come and meet my husband." He dropped into a whisper. "Harry doesn't like to travel, but when he heard a First Uploader was coming, he could hardly contain himself."

I nodded and squared my shoulders, aware of the scrutiny of hundreds of people and many media drones. "Lead on, Kwame."

Harry bowed very formally, then shyly presented me with flowers. Kwame insisted we pose for an "official" photo, as if there weren't already hundreds of images of us being shared across the world.

After that, the pair formed a cheerful and efficient vanguard, forging a path through the crowd that filled the tarmac and the grounds beyond. Urgent messages and requests filled up my dashboard, and I had to pause and update my privacy filter.

Fortunately, Kwame himself had chosen that moment to point out the antique electric hearse coming up the road. It stopped near us, and when they opened the rear doors, I was surprised to see what appeared to be a scale model of the *Adiona*.

"It's all the rage here," said Harry, his thick Scottish accent a bit difficult to follow. "They like to come up with a coffin which represents the deceased. Or something just whimsical."

Kwame said, "My great aunt was very fond of ginger ale, so they buried her in a replica of a giant soda bottle."

I chuckled. A moment later, *Dutchman* pinged me images of other Ghanian coffins: athletic shoes, biscuit jars, beer cans, and yes, fizzy drink bottles.

"When I asked the family about the interment," Kwame said, "everyone had different ideas. In the end, though, we all agreed this suited her."

"It does indeed," I said.

We watched them transfer Kakra's body into the coffin, and then into the hearse. Someone began singing. Other voices soon joined in. It wasn't long before the air was dense with music.

I closed my eyes, letting it wash over me. Awusi used to sing when she worked in the garden.

Sometimes I'd come home and sneak around the side gate so I could listen without disturbing her. She'd perform snippets of American gospel music, or Cambodian harvest chants, or even the occasional Billy Holiday tune. She often encouraged me to join her, and I always refused. I didn't want to dilute that beautiful sound with my own untrained voice. *What are you afraid of?* she'd ask. *Music is an extension of your heart.*

Now, surrounded by strangers under the hot sun, I think I understood. This was an extended family, sharing their grief and joy, and shouting it to the heavens. When the song broke into a call and response, I switched on a translator.

Our daughter has come home!
Yes, she is here, hey!

Look, there is another daughter!
Yes, there is.
Yes, there is.

All our daughters have come home!

In one corner of my message feed, a notification flashed a priority icon from Raadhi. I focused at it.

Have to see a man about a book. Promised to be there late tonight.

The funeral started the next day with a casual breakfast. I presented Kwame with Raadhi's coffee, which he immediately sent it to the kitchen. "All the coffee in the world started here in Africa," he said. "However, I will absolutely keep an open mind."

It was *very good* coffee.

The actual internment took up most of the morning, and then we had a formal meal and entertainment. They seated me at the head table, where I was introduced to dozens of Awusi's relatives. While neither Kakra nor her sister had produced children, their brother Táwia had fathered four, two of whom were present via avatar. The lack of lightspeed delay told me their physical bodies were housed somewhere nearby, maybe in the Pyrenees vaults. And the entertainment! Dancers and singers, and even storytellers, who presented creation myths and re-enacted family events, many of which centered around the sisters.

Kakra and her sister had, according to one fellow, engaged in a series of footraces and contests of strength to see who would be the first to ask out the most eligible girl in their school. Ataá Pánin was stronger, but Kakra faster. Eventually, Kakra had prevailed.

"Is this true?" I whispered to Kwame, after the storyteller sat down.

"The way I heard it the *loser* had to go out on the date. They were both very shy at that age."

I laughed and raised my glass of distilled palm wine, which the locals called *akpeteshie*. I hadn't much cared for it the first time Awusi served it; now though, it felt right: raw and passionate. It burned a path through my sadness, leaving only happy ashes.

"Quite the spectacle," said Raadhi, slipping into the chair next to me.

"I was wondering where you'd gotten to."

"I bumped into my old friend Ryan, if you can believe it. He and I did elephant population surveys in Gujarat, oh, thirty years ago." She pointed to another table of raucous guests under a sun sail that flexed with the breeze. "He's producing an Overmind play and one of the actors lives here. So naturally they invited the entire crew."

"Small world," I said.

"Perhaps," she said. "I think that after a hundred years, if you haven't checked into a vault, your social circle becomes set. Your hobbies or profession attract the same general group of people all moving in similar orbits. Our brains are happier when our social circles are manageable."

Similar orbits. Sure. It was something Awusi seemed to avoid. She'd go in one direction for a decade or two, then change vectors. Except for her writing. Even back in the lab, she kept a notebook full of ideas, scraps of overheard conversation, even drawings. I still had some random pages tucked away in a locker aboard *Dutchman*.

A very handsome woman approached our table and offered us tiny cakes and of course, more *akpeteshie*. Raadhi took a cake but covered her glass. "No more, please."

I raised my eyebrow. "Afraid to let your hair down?"

"Seems more like a party than a funeral to me." She looked around. "My parents were traditional Hindus. Funerals were pretty solemn affairs."

"This is like more like an Irish wake crossed with a family reunion," I said.

Kwame agreed. "We have always had great respect for our elders, and funerals became, well, something of a competition. Everyone tried to outdo each other. But when the Overmind came and people starting going into the vaults, everything changed."

"How so?" I asked.

"It's one thing to honor your grandfather for an entire weekend, but it's a different thing entirely when you run into him every time you transfer to an avatar."

I didn't have that experience. My *grootmoeder* was too old to participate in the Overmind: her limited neuroplasticity couldn't handle the link. As much as I wanted her to join the collective pool of minds, it just wasn't possible.

Before Hendrika went into hospice, we played a lot of cards, and I recorded all the family stories she had. Much of that data formed the basis of one of *Dutchman*'s subroutines.

"God, I miss her," I said, sniffling.

Raadhi handed me a napkin. "It's okay to cry at a funeral."

"It's not that." I wanted to explain I was thinking about my *grootmoeder*, but Kwame stood and gave a hearty shout.

"Quiet! Quiet, please!" He motioned to the band, "Thank you for the lovely music. Can we have a moment?" When the crowd settled down, he turned to me. "We are honored to have with us a special guest, M. Mylene Vandenberg." There followed applause and cheering that brought a deep blush to my cheeks. "But today she is not a guest. She is *family*, because she brought Kakra home to us." He gestured for me to stand. "Would you like to say something, Mylene?"

No. No. Absolutely not.

Then I heard *Dutchman* on my private channel. *You can do this, boss. I have faith in you.*

I stood, a little unsteady from both the wine and my anxiety. These people weren't here to listen to my music, or give me an award, or interview me about my work on the Overmind.

This wasn't my story.

It was *hers*.

"Good evening," I started. "Sorry, afternoon. I'm still on ship time." *Great start, Mylene.* "Thank you for inviting me."

Keep going, said Dutchman.

Right. "This is very difficult for me. When I stumbled upon Kakra, I thought I had found a piece of history, something valuable yet forgotten. In a way, I had, but I was also wrong. Even though no one was looking for the life pod, it didn't mean the body inside—the *person* inside—had been forgotten."

"While Kakra may have been alone out there, she was *never* forgotten. She belonged to this family, and to all of us."

Dutchman showed me live feed stats. Traditional cultural events like this drew decent audiences, but the presence of two members of the First Uploaders team and a mysterious corpse lost in time had spiked interest beyond expectation. Millions of people were watching, interacting with this event. I dismissed the window. I didn't want to think about that now.

"Like many siblings, Kakra and her sister competed with each other throughout childhood, and when they reached adulthood their competition led them to space. When Ataá Panin left this world, it was natural Kakra would follow her, if only to find a new prize they might wrestle over.

"Yet Ataá Panin didn't complete her journey, and that was something Kakra couldn't abide. When the *Abeona* arrived at the last known position of the *Khonsu*, Kakra decided to be with her sister a final time." I didn't know if my deduction was correct, though it seemed reasonable. "One night, Kakra waited until her crewmates were asleep, then used her interface to steal away in a life pod." I smiled. "It probably wasn't the first time she'd slipped away in the night to chase down her sister." Kwame chuckled next to me.

"When I found Kakra between the stars, I wanted to turn her story into an art exhibit, or perhaps an education project. That was...a mistake." I reached down for my wine glass.

In that moment, everything came into sharp focus. I knew what I had to say.

"I was grieving my own loss, and my grief blinded me."

Standing as straight as I could, I said, "Kakra's story is not mine to tell. She is not an art project, and she is not some historical object to be auctioned off to a museum. She is part of a family." I turned to Kwame.

"A family that has welcomed me as one of its own."
There was applause and cheers. I pushed on, "More importantly, my new relation Kwame has reminded me we are *all* family. We are all children of Earth. And now a lost child has come home."

I raised my glass. "To Kakra Danso-Sika."

The crowd raised their glasses and drank, then someone called for a song. The band started up, and people jumped to their feet.

Raadhi squeezed my shoulder and whispered, "That was lovely, Mylene. Now I'm going to dance." She offered her hand to Kwame.

Dutchman pinged me. *Are you all right, boss?*

Mostly, I replied. And in that moment, it was true.

So you're not going to sell the life pod.

No. No, I'm not.

We'll figure something out. When are you coming home?

Ask me tomorrow, I replied, taking my seat. A very old woman with bright eyes glanced my way and nodded in approval. She reminded me of Hendrika.

I sat there until I drifted off. Raadhi gently shook me awake, then walked me back to the little guest cottage they'd loaned us for the occasion. She helped with my dress and made me drink a large glass of water before rolling me onto the bed.

"You're stronger than you look," I said, yawning.

"It helps when you deal with rhinos," she replied.

Awusi had published her first book of poetry before we became lovers. I read it and enjoyed it. Unlike the critics, I didn't try to assign any hidden meanings behind her Earth Mother/Gaia imagery. I suspected she was simply processing her first *virtu* experience in her own way.

We were living together by the time she wrote her first autobiography, and she used to leave notes and draft pages all around the house. Still, she didn't want me to read anything until it was edited. That was tough. I learned to dust circumspectly and thought about Hendrika and mouse sneezes.

When a carton of books arrived one Saturday, I asked her if I could read one.

"It's only an advance reader copy," she said. "It's not the final product."

"I see. Will there be substantial changes?"

"No! At least, I hope not."

"Then there's no reason I can't read it, is there?" I said. "I promise not to circle any mistakes."

"Actually, it would be helpful if you did." She kissed me, handed me a copy, and retreated to the kitchen to bake bread.

I spent the whole afternoon on the couch, fascinated by Awusi's attention to detail—how many deciliters of coffee she drank on any given day—yet confused by her clinical detachment when she described her first upload.

She'd obviously pulled the lab records, listing the exact equipment in the room, the build of the software. There was also a clear timeline from when she arrived at work that day to her post-return examination by the neurologist.

She had even remembered the stain on my lab coat from a leaky pen. But there was nothing about her vision. No mention of the Goddess.

"Where did the poet go?" I asked her over bowls of butternut squash soup and thick slices of fresh bread.

"Right here," she said, raising her wine glass.

"But not *here*." I held up her autobiography. "This is very good, and I think you're going to have even more fans when people start reading it. But to be honest, I'm a little hurt."

"Oh?"

I toyed with my own wine glass. "When you came back, you breached the surface like a pearl diver, and I caught a glimpse of the *real* you, a woman who had experienced something phenomenal. And yet you glossed over it."

"Oh Mylene." She reached for my free hand. "I don't know exactly what happened when we made that first backup, but it touched me on a deep and spiritual level. It was intensely personal and private."

"Yet you wrote a whole book of poetry about it."

"Guilty," she admitted. "I thought poems could help me wrap my head around the whole thing."

"Did they?"

"A little. What helped a *lot* more was you." She squeezed my fingers. "You were there when it happened, and you're here now. That's all that matters."

We never got to dessert.

Even filtered through the curtains, the tropical sunlight was enough to drag me out of a deep sleep. I blinked and saw a note sitting on the nightstand next to a carafe of water and several hangover pills.

I unfolded the note. *Gone to the market. Back soon. —R*

"Bless you, Raadhi," I whispered before I swallowed the pills with several glasses of water. Then I carefully propped myself up on hand-stitched pillows and waited for the drugs to take effect.

I keyed my comm. "*Dutchman?*"

"Yes, Mylene."

"Anything important happen while I was out?"

"The funeral attracted a lot of attention. People are having real conversations, not just commenting," said *Dutchman*. "It might be wise to start thinking about a tour when you're done in Ghana, especially if you're serious about not selling the life pod."

"I can't sell it. Not after meeting her family."

"Then will you think about a tour?"

I know Dutchman was looking out for my financial health (and his maintenance), but it felt ghoulish to use this occasion to revive my career. I heard the front door open quietly. "We'll talk later," I said and then, "I'm awake!" I pulled on a robe and took careful steps to the little kitchen. Raadhi was filling a kettle. Her shopping bag sat on the counter.

"Good morning. How are you doing?" she said.

"Pretty good, all things considered." My stomach growled.

"Glad to hear." She put the kettle on stove. "I have something for you."

"Please say it's coffee."

"Maybe some rooibos this morning. It's good for your digestion." She smiled and pulled down a tea pot and mugs from the cupboard. From her shopping bag, she produced a bag of loose-leaf red tea. "I had a call from one of my favorite booksellers in Paris last week. Somehow he got hold of one of Awusi's sketchbooks."

"So that's what you were talking about. Did you buy it?"

"Not at the price he wanted!" The kettle began to whistle and she scooped leaves into the pot. "However, I was willing to negotiate once he showed me what was inside." She poured water over the tea, then reached into her shopping bag. "Here."

It was an envelope of heavy cream paper. One corner was loose. My name was printed across the front in the beautiful, distinctive cerulean ink that Awusi loved. I stared at it for a long time.

"I asked the dealer if he'd read the contents, and he said he hadn't since it was worth more with the original seal intact. I told him I believed him. I also let him know if a single sentence appeared in the public without your approval I would drop him naked in the Serengeti during the wildebeest migration." Raadhi filled her mug.

"It's a lovely morning," she said, "I think I will take my tea on the porch."

I nodded and waited for her to leave, then slipped a finger under the envelope's edge.

My dearest Mylene,

I pressed the paper to my face and inhaled sharply, catching a hint of her favorite bath oil.

It is particularly difficult to write this. I can't say "I am dead" because obviously that isn't true. I also can't say "I will be dead" because the universe doesn't care about our plans. Uncertainty principle? Shit happens.

Instead, let me say: **I'm sorry.**

Goddess, I'm tempted to write that over and over until I fill the paper, and it wouldn't be enough.

I **am** *sorry I am leaving you behind.*

All of you.

But especially you. You are the person I loved and respected and who gave me absolute unconditional love.

Even if we couldn't stay married.

I've done everything I wanted to do in this life. I want to see what comes next. Ever since the first time I transferred, I knew there was something else.

Please don't think I'm planning on killing myself because I'm depressed. Far from it.

I love my life and all the amazing things — and people — I've encountered along the way.

I am not afraid of dying. Who could be? Come on! You don't **know.** *It's silly to fear what you don't know. It's the devil you know that can really fuck you up.*

I realized some time ago I was never invested in becoming an ancestor. Which is strange, considering how much my family venerated their ancestors. On the other hand, I never did follow my parents' wishes.

*But **you** are an ancestor, Mylene. You just don't know it. I do. So please, find someone special and make some babies. Give them all the love I know you have.*

Every time I connect to the Overmind I hear whispers of love and laughter. Call it Gaia or Asase Yaa or whatever. Every time, I try to drink it all down into my heart. But I can't.

There's only one thing left to do. I'm going to go to Her.

I love you.

Your Awusi

I put the paper aside. Then I blew my nose.

After the funeral, I asked Kwame if he could find someone to manage a small foundation for me. He agreed and stayed on for a few days to hash out the details. He even recorded some voiceovers for the first exhibit in the planned Danso-Sika Family Museum.

"I have a confession," I said as we watched the life pod being eased into a storage shed on the newly leased property.

Kwame turned to me. "This is all an elaborate prank?"

"Of course not."

"That's good, because I would never be able to face my husband again if it were. And I'm flying home tomorrow." Then he smiled. I was going to miss his smile. "You are welcome to stay, if you wish. Family is always welcome."

"That means a lot," I said. "I might even take you up on it if I didn't already have plans." I needed to visit the cemetery in Ogooué-Ivindo before heading to Paris.

"The offer remains," he said. "So what is your confession?"

"I confess I don't understand Kakra's name. Her parents called her that because she's a twin, right?

"That's correct."

"She was born second, yet people refer to her as the *elder* twin."

"Ah, I can see your confusion," he said. "There is a belief among the Ankan people that when two children share the same womb, one is always a *little* more mature than the other. That child stays behind to make sure the other one gets out safe."

"Wait. They *help* them?"

"In a manner of speaking. From your perspective, Kakra is the younger sibling since she was born five or six minutes after. But we believe she is actually *older* since she was born second. I suspect she took her name very seriously and saw herself as her sister's protector."

"I think I see." I thought back on my brother, and how often I believed he was right because he was a whole year older. How would I have felt if the difference were only minutes?

"Excellent. Any other questions?"

"No." I shook my head. "Hold on, I have something for you." I dug through my pockets until I found the note from the life pod. "It was in Kakra's shipsuit."

He unfolded it and smiled again. "Thank you very much, Mylene."

"As much as I'd like to keep it, I think it should stay here with her."

He carefully tucked the note away.

The delivery bot closed the shed and sent me a receipt. I offered Kwame a hug, which he accepted. "Take care of yourself, Kwame. Give Harry a hug for me."

"I shall, my friend. Travel lightly."

I rented an apartment in Accra with a decent piano and poured myself into practice while *Dutchman* arranged for a series of performances that were part concert, part storytelling. I played in small venues, and often parked myself at local pubs afterward to share drinks and memories with anyone who wanted to join.

My older works were discovered, and re-discovered, and my credit balance grew comfortable again.

I spent it all on medical equipment, pharmaceuticals, printer stock, and as many luxuries as I could think of. It was going to be years before I made planetfall again, even if I was going to spend most of the trip in cryosleep.

On New Year's Eve, I met Raadhi and Steven in Paris. We strolled the snowy streets of the 7th *arrondissement* under a full moon, reveling in the unexpected quiet.

I was pleased to see the Eiffel Tower was still standing and adorned with lights. I missed the Arc de Triomphe, though. Steven said the Overmind had voted to remove it, along with a number of other buildings, during a cultural edit a few years back. Too violent a symbol.

"Sometimes I worry people are abandoning *veritas*," he said. "There's more than a billion people in *virtu*, and that number is growing."

"So what happens when it surpasses the birth rate?" I asked.

"It already has," said Steven.

"It's not so bad," Raadhi said. "Fewer people means we can accelerate habitat restoration and re-speciation."

"Great. Lions in the park."

"Don't worry, Steven," Raadhi said. "It's going to take at least another century to remediate everything. You'll still be able to eat without some other apex predator nosing your plate."

"I'll hold you to that," he said, winking at a passerby.

"Who's that?" I asked.

"Reynauld."

"Steven's husband. Lead actor of Toronto Shakespeare," said Raadhi.

I turned to Steven. "Why didn't you invite him to join us?"

Steven shrugged. "It's complicated."

"Trouble in paradise?" Raadhi asked.

"Oh no, nothing like that."

"Then what?"

"It's my Christmas present."

When we pressed him for details, he said that when he'd told his family about our little reunion, they'd insisted on running interference for us. His spouses, their siblings, and the rest of the extended family had quietly laid siege to the capital. It was a casual cordon that allowed us to experience the city without the obvious isolation of a privacy bubble.

"We're the last of the team," he said. "I wanted it to be... special."

Raadhi slipped her arm through his. "I always knew you were a romantic."

He blushed. Or it might have been the cold wind nipping his cheeks.

We found a café, ordered hot drinks, and spent several lovely hours catching up. Mostly, though, we shared stories of Awusi: her poetry, her dancing, her creative interpretation of deadlines, and her astonishing gift for inedible lasagna.

"She never really understood cheese," I said. A passing human server stopped and asked if we needed help with the menu. Our burst of laughter sent her scurrying off to another table.

The café's owner came by with a bottle of brandy and three snifters. "For the First Uploaders," he said, and poured for us.

After the owner left, Steven said, "See, there are some advantages to fame."

"I agree," said Raadhi. "Speaking of which, I read about your tour. *Dutchman* said it was quite successful."

"You've been talking with my ship?"

"It ordered a suspiciously large amount of tea and coffee," she said. "Going somewhere?"

"Rocannon," I replied. "I also ordered a surgical bot, pharmaceuticals, printer stock, and as many luxuries as I could think of. Even though I'll be in cryosleep for most of the way, I wanted to make sure the cupboards were full."

"Why now?" asked Steven. "You could have left whenever you wanted."

I rolled my snifter between my fingers. "I know. I thought about it, but every time I did, I couldn't do it. Couldn't leave her. Or Earth. To be honest though, this doesn't feel like home any more. It's time for someplace new." Then I mentioned that Awusi had thought of me as an ancestor. "I think I'm up for the challenge."

"That's why you're installing a surgical bot," said Raadhi.

"Just a precaution," I said.

"Okay, you lost me," said Steven.

I laughed at his expression. "We inserted Awusi's DNA into some donor sperm. *Dutchman* is keeping an eye on it as we speak."

"You couldn't ask for a better babysitter," said Raadhi.

When the church bells rang in the New Year and holographic fireworks filled the sky, I hugged and kissed them both, then headed back to my hotel. I slept with the windows open, burrowed under blankets.

I didn't remember my dreams, but I woke happy.

"Kobina, lunch!"

She came barreling into the kitchen. I caught her around the waist, converting her momentum into a twirl that dropped her into her chair.

Hendrika, strapping Johan into his highchair, sighed. "I wish you wouldn't encourage her, Mylene." Johan gurgled and fussed until Hendrika gave him a bamboo bowl of mashed potatoes, which he immediately plunged his hands into.

"But *grootmoeder*, I didn't knock over the water pitcher."

"This time, young lady."

Kobina's "grandmother" was a bespoke android masquerading as an elderly woman, right down to the varicose veins, creaky knees, and flabby arms. The neighbors treated her with respect due to her apparent age and uncanny ability to drink our strongest farmhands under the table.

"Speaking of water." I held out my glass. Kobina picked up the blue porcelain pitcher and filled my glass halfway using more grace than I ever had at seven. That was Awusi's genetic contribution, I was sure.

"Thank you."

"You're welcome, mama."

Hendrika nodded her approval and spooned up warm vegetables and cold salad. There was also sliced ham and pickled herring, or what passes for herring on Rocannon.

The planet was settled by Free Thinkers, a confluence of philosophers, artisans, and religious adherents who fled Earth once the Overmind reached critical mass.

Once they arrived, the Rocannonites dismantled their ships and set up a comfortable society, free from the background noise (and surveillance) of the Overmind.

There was a knock at the door.

"I'll get it!"

"No, I'll get it," I said. "It's business."

"How do you know?" said Kobina.

"Because this is *my* house and I know *everything* that goes on." I leaned forward and gently tapped her beautiful little nose.

"Mama!"

"I thought it was because you asked Joey Robertson to come by and give you an estimate for some construction," said Hendrika.

"That, too," I said and winked at my daughter. "Now after lunch, I want you to practice. Your Mozart is really coming along." We had an old electric keyboard set up in the spare bedroom. "Hendrika, can you watch the baby for just a minute?"

"I'll watch him paint his face," she said. "Won't I, little man?"

Joey doffed his sun hat when I opened the door, revealing lots of untidy blond hair. "Afternoon, Ms. Blikslager."

"Afternoon, Joey. Please call me Mylene."

"Not while I'm working."

"You're quick enough to call me Mylene when you're drinking my beer."

"That's *after* work," he said. "Different rules."

I took him to the side of the house, passing a small shrine. When Kobina was little, we had a little ceremony, the three of us, filling an urn with ashes from Awusi's grave on Earth. We said no prayers and released no lanterns. We did, however, drink sweet tea and eat little cakes. *Your mother watches over us*, I said.

"Here." I pointed to the wall. "I'd like to put in a set of French doors to get more light."

"There'll be some noise from the road, even with double panes."

"I think we can extend the line of clumping bamboo to deal with the worst of it." Not that there was much traffic, at least compared with my memories of Amsterdam.

He took measurements and made notes. "I'm doing a job for Mrs. Volkova right now. How soon do you need this?"

"Six weeks?" I glanced around and lowered my voice. "I want to make Kobina a proper music room for her summer solstice gift."

Joey adjusted his hat. "Well, in that case, I'll give you a discount as my contribution."

"I won't hear of it," I said. I still had a sizable stash of life extension meds and chocolate after buying the farm. "However, if you do a *really* good job, I'll see you get sneak peak of the new pilsner."

"I'll call you when I've framed the door. Good day to you, Ms. Blikslager."

"And to you, Joey."

There are no ansible connections on Rocannon. At least, none they know about.

In the basement of my farmhouse, amid the jars of dried fruit and spare solar panels, there sits an old can of paint, dented and rusty along the lid. Hidden in the false bottom is a personal narrow-band transceiver connected to *The Flying Dutchman*, which floated in synchronous orbit around Rocannon's second moon. If necessary, I could have the ship relay messages to Earth, though so far I haven't felt the need to do that. It's comforting to know I have the option.

Even with the help of Hendrika and a couple of strong young workers, it's a lot of work running a farm and raising two children. Especially one as wild as my little girl. I named her *Kobina* since she was born on a Tuesday. Her school records list her as Kobina Awusi Blikslager.

Johan came along later. I had a brief affair with a hydrologist named Conrad who wasn't interested in children, but wasn't adverse to contributing his DNA. On a colony as small as Rocannon, the joke goes, every has a duty to serve on a jury and diversify the gene pool. Conrad and I are still friends.

In a place like Rocannon, my children are free to be whoever they want. I taught Kobina about soil and chickens and how to program the very stupid machines we allowed ourselves. She taught me about climbing trees and jumping into cold ponds and how to laugh without restraint. Johan reminds me about the importance of naps.

Even without the Overmind, my children will live long and healthy lives, and their triumphs and mistakes will be their own. Their art, whatever form it takes, will live on after them, or not.

Once Joey finishes his work, I plan to send Kobina off to friend's house for a sleepover and call *Dutchman*. The ship has assured me its drones can manage the cargo, and this stretch of road is strong and straight enough for the shuttle. I've made a mental note to warn the neighbors about the landing. Johan will be thrilled. He liked loud noises, just like his namesake.

I can't wait to see Abina's face when she opens the doors and sees the piano.

Acknowledgments

As cliche as it sounds, "No one writes a book on their own" is a universal truth. I certainly didn't. Plenty of folks helped me along this journey: the amazing instructors, house elves, and students of **Viable Paradise XVI** (Fire Wombats); the cool kids of **Paradise Lost** in San Antonio; the **Rambo Academy for Wayward Writers**; **Codex**; my own writing group, **Genre Word Miners (with Cats & Dinos)**; plus the numerous pro writers, editors, and beta readers who provided me feedback and encouragement along the way.

A special shout-out to Mark Bilsborough at **Wyldblood Press** who gave this story a home and graciously allowed me to track him down at the Glasgow Worldcon so we could talk business.

My wife must also be included in any list. Without her support, I would have quit this whole thing years ago.

Karl Gustav Dandenell
Alameda, California
December 2025

Karl Dandenell is a graduate of Viable Paradise and a Full Member of the Science Fiction & Fantasy Writers Association. He and his family, plus their feline overlords, live on an island near San Francisco famous for its Victorian architecture and low-speed traffic. Karl has published over 50 works of short fiction in the United States, Canada, and Great Britain. Follow his occasional posts @karldandenell.bsky.social and read more about of his fiction at www.firewombats.com.